# Santa's Tatty Old Boots

To Addison

by Sherry Baldwin

illustrated by Karel Hayes and John Gorey

ISBN 13: 978-1-937721-37-4
Library of Congress Control Number: 2016948547


Published by
Peter E. Randall Publisher
5 Greenleaf Woods Drive #102, Portsmouth, NH 03801
www.perpublisher.com


Copies are available from:
Enfield Distribution
www.enfieldbooks.com


Book Design: Grace Peirce


Composed and printed in The United States of America

It was Christmas Eve night and time to get dressed.
Santa Claus wanted to look his best.

Outside he could see the northern lights glow,
so he pulled on his boots to walk in the snow.

But his boots were worn out,
at the tip was a hole,

and his big toe stuck out,
above the black sole.

"In these tatty old boots,
there's one thing I know,
I'll freeze off my toes
in the ice and snow!"

So he called for his
elves, and lickety-split,
they came on the run
and told him to sit!

Santa tried elf shoes, in red, green, and blue,
but elf shoes are pointy and just wouldn't do.

Then he looked in his closet at all of his shoes,
and thought about weather and which pair to choose.

Well, slippers are nice and warm for a ride,
but slippers are shoes you should wear inside.

Next he took flip-flops down from the shelf,
and flip-flopped around enjoying himself.
"But flip-flops are no good in snow," said an elf.

Blue bowling shoes are great for a game.
They've got Santa style, but all the same,
he started to slip, and those shoes were to blame!

The elves thought roller skates might be all right,
but Santa was not used to rolling at night.

Then he tried shoes
that were festive and funky,
but he tripped on the tree
because they were clunky.

Mrs. Claus brought her boots for Santa to try,
but her boots were so tight they made Santa cry.

"I know! Let's mend my old boots!" Santa said.
So Mrs. Claus got her ribbons, a needle, and thread.

The elves added tape. The reindeer brought glue . . .

. . . and soon Santa's boots
were better than new!

He thanked Mrs. Claus, with a smile on his face,
and hopped on his sleigh with the reindeer in place.

"These tatty old boots always fit me just right . . ."

"... Now they'll keep my toes warm
on Christmas Eve night!"